GREEN-COLLAR CAREERS

RE-GREENING THE ENVIRONMENT

CAREERS IN CLEANUP, REMEDIATION, AND RESTORATION

By Suzy Gazlay

CRABTREE
Publishing Company
www.crabtreebooks.com

Crabtree Publishing Company

Author: Suzy Gazlay
Publishing plan research and development:
  Sean Charlebois, Reagan Miller
  Crabtree Publishing Company
Editors: Mark Sachner, Molly Aloian
Proofreader: Crystal Sikkens
Editorial director: Kathy Middleton
Photo research: Ruth Owen
Designer: Westgrapix/Tammy West
Production coordinator: Margaret Amy Salter
Prepress technician: Margaret Amy Salter
Print coordinator: Katherine Berti
Production: Kim Richardson
Curriculum adviser: Suzy Gazlay, M.A.

Written, developed, and produced by Water
Buffalo Books

Photographs and reproductions:
Alamy: Jim West: page 23; Jeff Morgan: page 26 (right).
Corbis: Joaquin Morell: page 16; STR/epa: pages 36–37; Lee
Celano: page 39 (top); Ed Kashi: page 41 (top); Ed Kashi: page 41
(bottom); Bettmann: page 43; Bridget Besaw: page 52.
FLPA: Flip Nicklin: page 21; Oene Moedt: page 30; Imagebroker:
page 33; Michael Durham: pages 50–51 (main).
Molly Land: p. 20.
Sarrah Minnick/NPS Photo: page 1 (center); page 55 (top).
Lorraine Parsons/NPS Photo: page 54; page 55 (bottom);
page 58 (left center).
Science Photo Library: Robert Brook: page 6; Simon Fraser: page
14; Peter Yates: page 34 (right); Hazen Group, Lawrence Berkeley
National Laboratory: page 45 (top).
Shutterstock: cover; page 1 (top); pages 4–5 (main); page 4
(bottom); page 5 (bottom left); page 5 (bottom center); page 7;
page 8; page 9; page 11; page 13; page 15; page 17 (main); page 18;
page 19; page 22; page 24; page 25; page 26 (left); page 27; page
28; page 31; page 34 (left); page 35 (top); page 38; page 39
(bottom); page 42; page 45; page 47; page 53; page 56; page 57;
page 58 (left top); page 58 (left bottom); page 58 (right).
Jeff Tracy: page 5 (bottom right); page 10; page 17 (bottom right);
page 29; page 32; page 48.
Wikipedia Creative Commons (public domain): page 35; page 40;
page 46; page 50 (lower left).

Library and Archives Canada Cataloguing in Publication

Gazlay, Suzy
    Re-greening the environment : careers in cleanup, remediation, and
restoration / Suzy Gazlay.

(Green-collar careers)
Includes index.
Issued also in electronic format.
ISBN 978-0-7787-4858-8 (bound).--ISBN 978-0-7787-4869-4 (pbk.)

    1. Environmentalists--Vocational guidance--Juvenile literature.
2. Environmental engineers--Vocational guidance--Juvenile literature.
3. Environmental protection--Vocational guidance--Juvenile literature.
I. Title. II. Series: Green-collar careers

GE60.G395 2011   j363.7'0023   C2011-902883-2

Library of Congress Cataloging-in-Publication Data

Gazlay, Suzy.
 Re-greening the environment : careers in cleanup, remediation, and
restoration / Suzy Gazlay.
    p. cm. -- (Green-collar careers)
 Includes index.
 ISBN 978-0-7787-4858-8 (reinforced library binding : alk. paper) --
ISBN 978-0-7787-4869-4 (pbk. : alk. paper) -- ISBN 978-1-4271-9722-1
(electronic pdf)
1. Environmentalists--Vocational guidance. 2. Environmental engineers-
-Vocational guidance. 3. Environmental protection--Vocational guidance.
I. Title. II. Series.

GE60.G4 2011
363.70023--dc22

2011015635

Crabtree Publishing Company

www.crabtreebooks.com   1-800-387-7650

Printed in China/082011/TM20110511

Published in Canada
Crabtree Publishing
616 Welland Ave.
St. Catharines, Ontario
L2M 5V6

Published in the United States
Crabtree Publishing
PMB 59051
350 Fifth Avenue, 59th Floor
New York, New York 10118

Published in the United Kingdom
Crabtree Publishing
Maritime House
Basin Road North, Hove
BN41 1WR

Published in Australia
Crabtree Publishing
3 Charles Street
Coburg North
VIC 305

CONTENTS

WHAT DO YOU MEAN, RE-GREEN?

Engineer

Backhoe Operator

Ecologist

Technician

Does it make you angry when you see a pile of trash dumped by the side of the road? Does it bother you to see damage done to a wild area? Are you concerned about breathing polluted air or drinking polluted water?

Do You Want to Help?

Do you wonder what has happened to the animals that used to live in a field or woodland that has now been paved over? As you watch images of destruction from a natural disaster on the news, do you wonder how either the people or the places can ever recover?

Chemical pollution can have a devastating effect on both the sea and fresh water. The cleanup efforts needed to restore this shore area will extend to land and water alike.

Factories pour pollutants into the atmosphere. Construction projects dig into potentially contaminated soil and groundwater. Deadly chemical pollution fouls our waterways. Our trash is destroying natural wildlife habitats. The need to put people to work on re-greening the environment has never been greater!

Researcher

Most of all, do you want to be able to do something about these problems?

If so, you might want to think seriously about a career in which you could help the environment recover from damage it has suffered. It's an important challenge. Our health depends upon the health of the environment in which we live. When even a small part of the environment is damaged or destroyed, the effect can go far beyond that one place.

Hydrogeologist

CAREER PROFILE

CLEANING UP COMPOUNDS IN SOIL AND GROUNDWATER: HYDROGEOLOGIST

Let's say a gas station is sold. The owners must demonstrate that their property meets state contamination standards. If it doesn't, the soil and groundwater must be remediated. That's where environmental services people like me and those I work with come in.

My main job is managing projects that investigate the extent of soil and groundwater contamination and identify what (such as drinking water) will be affected by contaminants. I then work with clients to develop and implement cleanup strategies.

I work mostly in an office, but I'm often out in the field. Right now, I have an office on a project site in Wisconsin. I like being able to help clients prevent environmental problems from developing in the future. I also enjoy mentoring younger staff members so they can advance in their careers.

My job gives me the chance to be creative in how I solve remediation problems. I have a bachelor's degree in Geology, but I work with people in engineering, environmental science, and even finance.

Together, we use our different points of view to help people, businesses, and the environment!

Jeff Tracy
Senior Hydrogeologist, Project Manager
AECOM (Milwaukee office)
Los Angeles, California

5

These tree saplings protected inside plastic tubes are part of an urban reforestation project in Ellesmere Port, Cheshire, UK. The goal of the project is to increase the area covered by forested land from 4 percent in 2000 to 30 percent by 2025.

How "Re-Greening" Works

Re-greening means doing whatever is necessary to remediate (clean up) and restore a damaged area, large or small. It also means getting the area back to a natural, healthy state. Successful re-greening would not be complete without taking steps to be sure that the area stays healthy. The area needs ongoing monitoring to be sure that all is well. Its resources must be used wisely and not used up, or depleted.

There are countless exciting possibilities and opportunities for people who would like to make re-greening the environment their life work. In this book, you'll see what is being done about some of the many types of events that affect the health of this planet. You'll also read about some of the different jobs involved. Perhaps they will give you ideas for careers in remediating and restoring the environment.

Where Do You Fit in?

Re-greening takes time and work. Whether the damaged area is large or small, many different skills are needed to restore the health of the environment. Does being a supervisor or manager appeal to you? Are you an "idea person," good at thinking of ways to solve problems? How about organizing people or raising funds? Perhaps you are already really good at teamwork and like the idea of working with others to make something happen. Are you willing to literally dig in with a shovel or operate heavy equipment? These are just two of the typical jobs that are part of a re-greening project.

BP oil workers attempt to clean an oil-covered beach on June 23, 2010, in Pensacola Beach, Florida. The oil was deposited following the massive BP disaster in the Gulf of Mexico.

ECOSYSTEMS—BALANCE IS ESSENTIAL

An ecosystem includes everything living and nonliving in a certain area on land or in water. Everything in the ecosystem interacts with and depends on each other. Some organisms will eat and others will be eaten. The ecosystem provides food, water, air, shelter, and space for those that live there. In a balanced ecosystem, some members of each species will survive and reproduce.

An ecosystem can become unbalanced because of pollution, significant temperature change, and habitat loss or destruction. Other causes include the loss of native plants and animals or the invasion of an organism that does not belong. A disaster such as a mudslide or wildfire can also destroy the balance.

There is a huge demand for experts who understand the environment and know how to help restore natural places. An interest in science, as well as math and technology, could lead you into a broad field of science such as ecology (study of organisms and the environment). Perhaps you might want to specialize in an area such as insects, bacteria, or water quality. You could do research or investigate the source of environmental problems. You may be the one who comes up with solutions or monitors a restored area. There are so many possibilities for someone who wants to make a difference in re-greening the environment!

You may think this is just a picture of some trees. It's actually part of a vast woodland ecosystem that is home to trees, mosses, and other plants, as well as various types of fungi, small mammals, birds, and millions of insects.

SCIENCE SPECIALISTS

Most scientists begin by studying everything they can about math, technology, and science in general. Then, usually in graduate programs, they focus on a specialty that will lead to their life's work.

Here are some of the science specialties that might be needed on re-greening projects and in some of the jobs that are discussed in this book:

ENVIRONMENTAL SCIENCES:

- Conservation biology—keeping diversity (variety) in nature, especially through the protection of habitats, ecosystems, and environments
- Ecology—relationships between living things and their surroundings
- Environmental chemistry—chemical and biochemical events in nature
- Environmental geology—solving environmental problems related to earth science (geology)
- Environmental soil science—interaction of human activity and soil
- Green chemistry—reduction of potential pollution at its source
- Toxicology—symptoms, detection, and treatment of poisons affecting living things

BIOLOGY—LIVING THINGS:

- Marine biology—saltwater organisms
- Freshwater biology—organisms in freshwater ecosystems
- Zoology—animals
- Botany—plants
- Microbiology—living things too small to be seen without magnification

ENGINEERING:

- Bioengineering—use of living systems to solve problems such as spills and waste
- Chemical engineering—better products, cleaner technology
- Environmental engineering—ways to protect the environment

GEOLOGY—EARTH SCIENCE:

- Hydrogeology—groundwater in soil and rocks
- Hydrology—water
- Limnology—inland waters
- Pedology—soil

OTHER FIELDS

- Population dynamics—short- and long-term changes in populations
- Statistics—collection, organization, interpretation of data
- Technology—use of technological equipment and systems

DON'T BREATHE THE AIR! DON'T DRINK THE WATER!

I f there was ever a time to get serious about cleaning up our environment, it's now. We know enough to recognize the causes and effects of pollution. More than ever, we understand the seriousness of the impact on our health and on the natural world. The world needs a work force that will address pollution, work to reduce and prevent it, and even regain some of the ground that has been lost. It's a great time to think about being part of that team!

Remediating contaminated water is a team effort. After this water sample is collected, environmental engineers, hydrologists, toxicologists, and technicians will work together to determine the best plan to reduce contaminants in the water.

> "Water and air, the two essential fluids on which all life depends, have become global garbage cans."
>
> Jacques Cousteau,
> French ecologist, explorer, inventor, author, filmmaker, and photographer specializing in the sea and underwater life-forms

Air Pollution Isn't New

Air pollution has been around for centuries, especially since at least the 11th century, when people began burning coal instead of wood. In the mid-1700s, the Industrial Revolution began in Britain and spread to the rest of Europe and to North America. Coal-burning machines filled the air with smog and smoke. The world was forever changed, and society was on its way to its dependence on fossil fuels.

Air pollution is a serious global problem. It affects both human health and the health of our planet. Unfortunately, a lot of damage has already been done.

POLLUTION—IT'S EVERYWHERE!

Signs of pollution are all around us.

Power plants and factories belch out smoke.

Smog (thick, polluted air) hangs over our cities.

The ground beneath a gas station is contaminated by leaky storage tanks and splashes from customers topping off their tanks. When it rains, the sheen from spilled oil and gasoline on the pavement provides a hint of the contamination occurring below the surface.

A sewage spill closes several beaches along the coast.

Litter drifts across the road and catches in the bushes. The remains of an old car rust away at the edge of a pasture.

Homes, businesses, cars, and trucks burn fossil fuels, putting huge amounts of carbon dioxide (CO_2) into the air. It adds to the layer of smog hanging over the city.

FOSSIL FUELS

Millions of years ago, tiny water plants and animals died and sank to the bottom of rivers, lakes, and oceans. As time passed, they were buried beneath layers of sediments. Heat and pressure from thick rock layers changed their remains to oil and natural gas. Land plants were going through a similar process, but the result was coal.

Oil, natural gas, and coal are fossil fuels. They are convenient, and we thought they were abundant, so we've come to rely upon them as sources of power. At the rate we're using them, however, we'll probably run out within a hundred years.

When fossil fuels are burned, the carbon in them combines with oxygen to form carbon dioxide (CO_2). The CO_2 is released into the atmosphere, where it contributes to global warming. The only solution to this serious problem is to develop other sources of energy. We need to stop depending on fossil fuels.

We need to prevent air pollution, reduce the damage done, and try to reverse the effects. There is plenty of work to be done.

Air Pollution—An Unhealthy Mix

In the United States, the Environmental Protection Agency (EPA) has created an Air Quality Index (AQI) to rate the level of pollution. The AQI is based on six major pollutants: ground-level ozone, particulate matter, carbon monoxide, sulfur dioxide, nitrogen dioxide, and lead. Each of these pollutants is regulated by a law called the Clean Air Act. Canada and the UK (United Kingdom) have similar laws.

Ozone—good news, bad news. Ozone (O_3) is a colorless form of oxygen gas. It is either very good or very bad, depending on where it is. Up in the stratosphere, 6 to 30 miles (10–48 kilometers) above Earth's surface, a layer of ozone protects us from harmful radiation from the Sun. Down at ground level, it's a whole different story. Ozone forms from reactions between two major types of pollutants: volatile organic compounds (VOCs) and nitrogen oxides. VOCs come from gasoline pumps, chemical plants, print shops, and oil-based paints.

Like it or not, toxic chemicals are all around us. They affect our health, especially that of children. Asthma is a serious respiratory disease triggered by a combination of viruses, allergies, and exposure to polluted air. Here, a boy uses an inhaler to get relief from his asthma.

Nitrogen oxides are released by cars, power plants, industrial plants, and other sources. The reactions depend upon heat and sunlight. That's why smog is often worse in the summer.

Particulate matter—"air junk." Particulate matter is the solid "stuff" in the air. It's a mix of microscopic solids and liquid droplets suspended in the air. The solids are chemicals, metals, particles of soil and dust, pollen, mold, and soot. They come from fireplaces, power plants, industries, vehicles, and nature. Some of the larger particles are dust stirred up by traffic. Particle pollution can sometimes be seen as a haze. Like ozone, it is very unhealthy to breathe.

In 2010, New Delhi, India (shown here under a layer of smog), shared with Beijing, China, the distinction of having the worst air pollution on the planet.

Smaller amounts, still big problems. Carbon monoxide (CO), nitrogen dioxide (NO_2), sulfur dioxide (SO_2), and lead come from various sources. Most of these are the result of the burning of fossil fuels in vehicles, power plants, and other industries. They can cause a variety of health problems. These range from asthma and other respiratory problems to the reduction of oxygen in people's organs and tissues.

WHAT IS CLIMATE CHANGE?

Climate change, also called global warming, is the gradual increase in temperature that our planet is experiencing. Today, most scientists agree that this increase is caused by humans burning the fossil fuels oil and coal. Burning fossil fuels releases harmful gases, such as carbon dioxide (CO_2), methane, and nitrous oxide, into the atmosphere. These gases have become known as "greenhouse gases." This is because they trap heat from the Sun on Earth, just as the glass of a greenhouse traps heat.

Our planet needs heat and light in order for living things to exist. Too much heat can be a bad thing, however. Parts of the world may become too dry for food to grow. Weather may become more extreme, resulting in hurricanes, heat waves, and torrential rain. If this happens, glaciers and the giant ice caps at the north and south poles will melt. This would cause ocean levels to rise. Some scientists predict that if the ice in the planet's glaciers melts, ocean levels would rise by as much as 200 feet (61 meters), flooding coastal towns and cities.

Global Warming—Too Late to Remediate?

During the 20th century, the average global temperature rose by a little more than 1.0°F (0.6°C). Snow cover and sea ice decreased. Mountain glaciers retreated. Scientists say that these and other events indicate that climate change has already begun. They add, however, that it's not too late to slow it down and even turn it around. The career choices you make could put you right into the middle of the action!

The first step is to stop depending on fossil fuels. This is an exciting time to be involved in developing clean energy. Solar, wind, hydro, thermal, tidal, biofuels, and more—so many choices and possibilities! Depending upon your interests, you could be in a "think tank" brainstorming ideas, creating computer models, designing technology, and fine-tuning solutions.

Acid rain is a serious problem directly connected to air pollution. Gases from coal-burning power plants mix with water, oxygen, and other chemicals in the atmosphere. The result is a mix of sulfuric acid and nitric acids. Winds can blow these acids hundreds of miles before they land. They can come down as acidic rain, fog, or snow. The change they cause in rivers, lakes, and streams harms or even kills the plants and animals that live there. Acid rain can also harm human-made structures, such as this stone sculpture on a rooftop in Cracow, Poland. The effects of acid rain have worn holes into the face of the sculpture.

You could be building, installing, or monitoring actual energy systems. Are you interested in cars? Perhaps you'd like to be involved in designing a car powered by clean energy. If you are comfortable being in front of people, perhaps you'd like to work in sales, communication, or education.

These are just a few of the many possibilities in this rapidly expanding field. Climate change is a global problem, so becoming involved in solutions might also provide opportunities for travel.

CAREER PROFILE

PROMOTING WIND POWER: MANAGER IN GOVERNMENT RELATIONS

My job is to increase the use of wind power across Canada.

The company I work for builds wind turbines. Wind power is fairly new to a lot of people, so we have to educate them about its benefits. Wind power is a clean, renewable energy source.

I enjoy seeing wind turbines being built and people realizing their benefits. Wind power is a sustainable source of energy. It is safe for the environment and creates growth opportunities for the economy. The wind energy industry will continue to grow over the next decade with new developments in science, business, organization, and design.

If you are interested in a career in renewable energy, there are many options to consider. You could study science, engineering, policy, business, or finance. Volunteering with trade or industry organizations, such as the Canadian Wind Energy Association, will help you gain experience and become familiar with the industry.

Gary Pundsack
Manager, Government Relations
Vestas Canadian Wind Technology, Inc.
(Vestas Americas)
Toronto, Ontario

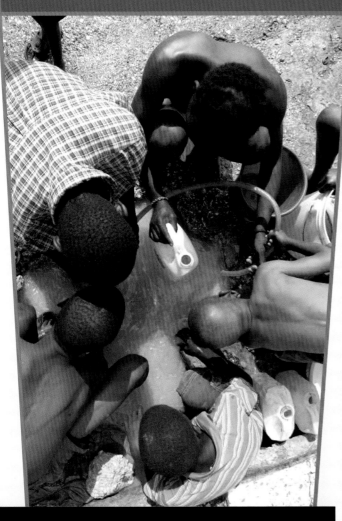

Haitians collect water from a leaking pipe in Port-au-Prince, the capital of Haiti, following a devastating earthquake in 2010. Water from unsafe sources such as this can carry the life-threatening disease cholera.

Troubled Waters

All living things, including human beings, need clean, uncontaminated water to live. Sadly, hundreds of people around the world die every day from drinking unclean water. The only water available to them is contaminated, and they need to drink it. The water may contain bacteria that cause diseases, or it may be polluted with toxic chemicals. Contaminated water may look clean, but it can cause illnesses or even death.

Nature Does It Well

In a balanced aquatic ecosystem, normal wildlife activity keeps water clean and safe for the inhabitants. It might not be safe drinking water for humans, but it's just right for the plants and animals in that ecosystem. Scavenging animals clean up debris on the bottom. Shade from nearby trees—or no shade at all—allows the system to maintain the perfect temperature for its inhabitants.

If something happens to the water, everything can change. Especially in an aquatic habitat, the inhabitants are very sensitive to even the smallest changes. If the change is serious enough, the habitat can be damaged or destroyed.

The algae covering this river may be the result of thermal pollution—a significant increase in the temperature of the water. The cause might also be organic pollution—fertilizer or farm waste running into the river. In either case, the thriving algae use up oxygen and block sunlight, killing off native plants, fish, and other organisms.

Threats to Underground Water

Rock formations called aquifers run underground, more or less parallel to the surface. Water soaks down through the soil until it reaches an aquifer. The water may collect in pools above the aquifer or move slowly along the aquifer through pores in the rock.

When a well is drilled, it reaches into the aquifer and pumps out water. If the water at the surface is polluted, these pollutants can seep down the borehole and into the aquifer. Once in the aquifer, the polluted water can spread further, affecting wells along the way. Pollution in one well can spread to other wells through the aquifer.

Down the Drain? Bad Idea!

Storm drains are for moving rainwater out of the street. That's all they are designed to do. These drains often lead to channels or streams.

This photo was taken at a site where hydrogeologists and other environmental scientists are testing and treating soil and groundwater. We can see from the "sheen" of this water being pumped into a bucket that it has been contaminated by oil leaching, or seeping, from the soil into the groundwater.

A landfill is a waste dump. If designed and used properly, landfills can be effective ways of preventing pollution from seeping through the soil and into groundwater. Most landfills have a thick plastic liner between the ground and the trash to keep the waste from getting into the aquifer. Every so often the trash is compacted, or pressed together, and a layer of soil is added. This helps control odor and pests.

Soap, bleach, or other household chemicals going down the storm drain may get into these waterways. They could also meet up with plants or animals along the way. The same goes for paint, oil, and just about anything else that isn't just plain water. When these substances spread through aquifers and other underground waterways, the results are devastating to the water supply. They are also harmful to any plant, animal, and human life that comes into contact with that water.

Publicizing Pollution Prevention

It seems simple enough, but many people have no idea of the harm they are doing by throwing all sorts of nasty stuff into the street, trash containers, or even their backyards. The best way to deal with this kind of threat is to prevent it, and publicity is the way to go. You might be the one to come up with a way to teach others. The next time a utility bill arrives, check out the inserts stuffed in the envelope with the bill. It's someone's job to produce those. If you have a creative side, you might be interested in writing, editing, graphic design, advertising, marketing, or Web site design. If so, then creating informational materials for print or online could be a great job for you.

Toxic Trouble

Many soaps, detergents, and other cleaning products contain toxic chemicals. The ingredients are listed on the container, but most people don't know what they are or how harmful they might be.

Working with members of a creative team of graphic designers, writers, editors, and Web designers can be a satisfying and enjoyable way of earning a living and bringing environmental awareness to the public.

Some contain pesticides and other chemicals known to cause cancer. Some are toxic to breathe or eat, but people don't realize it, so they spray them around food and on cooking surfaces. Janitors and other professional cleaners sometimes use cleaning products that are even more toxic!

It's important that we keep our homes, schools, and bodies clean and free of germs. However, the agents in certain cleaners are hazardous to both our health and the environment. Some cleaning agents evaporate into the air. Others get washed down drains. The vapors affect the air quality indoors and add to the formation of smog outdoors. Aquatic animals are especially sensitive to chemicals in the water in which they live. In fact, tests and observations have shown that some chemicals interfere with an animal's ability to reproduce. What's even more unsettling is that scientists have not yet discovered the long-term effects of many of these chemicals.

Green Cleaners

As consumers, we now have the option of buying a wide range of green cleaning agents. Not only are they safer for us, but they are also designed not to cause harm to the environment. Researchers and technicians are at work coming up with new and better products.

Perhaps you'll find a future career working to create some really effective green cleaners. You might want to start up a company to market green cleaning products or be part of the team behind such a company. Perhaps you want to be a part of a janitorial or cleaning service that uses only Earth-friendly products.

A toxicologist examines a pregnant Beluga whale that died in the Gulf of St. Lawrence, in Canada. Scientists believe that the whale, like other wildlife, may have been killed by toxic pollution caused by pesticides and other dangerous chemicals. These substances can reduce animals' ability to fight off infectious diseases.

CAREER PROFILE

CHEMICALS IN FISH: RESEARCH ASSOCIATE

I develop methods for finding chemicals in fish from our lakes and rivers. Some of the toxins I look for can cause cancer, hormone problems, and nervous system ailments in humans and animals.

Chemicals get into our water from industrial manufacturing, chemical processing, and electrical generating equipment. Even when handled safely, a small amount of a chemical can quickly contaminate a large area. Fish take in these chemicals simply by living in contaminated water.

On a typical day, I might prepare and purify fish samples. I try out different types of technology to get the most accurate results.

My university background includes a degree in Chemical Engineering. Then I worked for several years as an intern in an environmental laboratory.

I enjoy problem solving and doing new research. There are often technical difficulties getting these projects up and running. But once the problems are overcome, the results are very rewarding.

In the future, I hope to see more funding for research. I'd also like to see more sharing of information among agencies. This would lead to newer and more exciting ways of fighting water pollution.

Liad Haimovici
Research Associate
Brock University and
Ontario Ministry of the Environment
Toronto, Ontario

What about Hazardous Waste?

Hazardous waste management companies specialize in the collecting, storing, treating, and disposing of dangerous substances. These include used oil, pesticides, certain cleansing agents, refrigerants used in air conditioners and other cooling appliances, certain kinds of batteries, fluorescent light tubes, and products that contain mercury or other dangerous elements. Even some smoke detectors contain small amounts of radioactive elements and must be disposed of as radioactive waste!

Depending on the type of substance, hazardous materials may be stored in several different ways. Some are stored temporarily in sealed containers, such as large plastic or metal drums or in enclosed or open-topped tanks. Other options include containment buildings with no contact with other structures, underground structures lined with heavy plastic, or waste piles designed so the waste doesn't touch the ground.

Dangerous substances are also treated to make them less hazardous or to reduce their amount. They may also be transported to disposal sites, such as protected landfills or underground wells designed to handle waste.

Who works with hazardous waste? Hazardous waste management companies and other waste management companies provide jobs for a lot of different people. These people have different levels of training and expertise.

Used fluorescent tubes are collected for recycling. The tubes contain hazardous materials such as mercury. They must be disposed of or recycled carefully.

Trained employees include handlers, drivers, technicians, hydrogeologists, safety specialists, compliance managers, field chemists, engineers, machine operators, toxicologists, and more!

Global Opportunities

Plenty of agencies, organizations, and other groups are working on a global level to clean up, remediate, and restore troubled land and water ecosystems. Many of these groups focus on helping both people and the environment.

Do you like to travel? Are you interested in tackling re-greening projects in other countries? There are numerous job opportunities for you to explore. For example, global organizations such as the World Wildlife Fund (WWF) have field agents. Rather than working in an office, these employees live and work in different countries all over the world.

Also needed are people to head up and work on projects such as designing and installing clean water systems in villages where the water isn't safe to drink. If you are interested in politics, you'll find nations working together to negotiate global guidelines for land and water issues alike. Volunteering gives valuable experience and can lead to a career. A Peace Corps experience can include teaching environmental awareness and working on environmental issues in a host country. From earthquakes to hurricanes, floods, and tsunamis, both urgent and ongoing help are needed after a natural disaster just about anywhere in the world.

Young trainees dressed in HazMat gear (short for *Hazardous materials)* learn how to clean up hazardous materials at the Michigan Laborers' Training and Apprenticeship Institute. Their training is being provided by Job Corps, a program run by the U.S. Department of Labor that provides free job and career training for low-income teens.

LOVING THE LAND

D o you have a certain place outdoors where you like to go? Maybe it's a nearby park, a spot in your backyard, or a grove of trees in your neighborhood. When you go there, if you see a piece of trash, do you pick it up?

Pick It Up!

If you have a garden, you know what it's like to have a special piece of land to care for. People need to think of the environment in the same way. The natural world is there for all of us to enjoy. If you live in the city, you might have to look a little harder to find it, but it's there. Whether it's an overgrown lot, a small green triangle or square in the middle of the city, or a huge national park, every part of the environment is important to our health and well being.

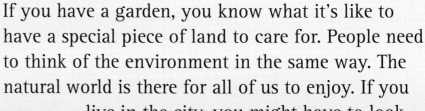

STOOP & SCOOP

PICK UP AFTER YOUR PET

Different kinds of litter create a variety of threats to safety and the environment. Dangerous broken glass on a beach can ruin someone's day or even inflict a serious injury. Fast-food packaging thrown from car windows litters roadsides and presents a choking danger to animals. Dog waste can make a mess of your shoes or even cause serious illness.

An all-too-familiar sight at beaches and public parks—garbage scattered around overflowing trash containers. Too often, trash left on the ground

It's likely you've been encouraged to pick up litter since you were a little kid. Many communities post notices and even fine people who get caught littering. Still, we see litter everywhere. There's a saying that "Beauty dies where litter lies." How true. One piece of trash immediately draws attention away from the rest of the landscape. It tends to be worse in public places and on roadways, but it can be found anywhere that people go—or where the wind blows it or water carries it.

Litter comes in many different forms and materials. It's both unsightly and costly to clean up. It may also be hazardous, attracting rodents and spreading germs. Trash piles burn quickly and can spread easily, and people and animals can get hurt by sharp objects or broken glass. Have you noticed how much trash is made up of fast-food packaging?

A volunteer cleans up litter at the side of a country road.

LITTER
CREW
AHEAD

ONE PERSON'S TRASH IS ANOTHER PERSON'S TREASURE

Here's one way to help the environment as a volunteer. A lot of the stuff going into landfills can still be used for other purposes. The Freecycle Network has a solution. Rather than dumping unwanted items, Freecycle members offer to give them away!

Freecycle has a number of local groups. Members of each group post offers by email or on a Web site. Other group members respond if they see something they can use. The original owner decides who gets it. Everything is run by volunteers. Typical postings include clothes, furniture, kitchen items, computer items, leftover paint, toys—just about anything!

Freecycle was founded as a local group in Arizona in 2003 and has grown rapidly. As of 2010, there were member groups in more than 85 countries. Every day they keep more than 500 tons (454 metric tons) of trash out of landfills. They say that they are "changing the world a gift at a time." Check it out at Freecycle.org!

The Three Rs: Reduce, Reuse, Recycle

We could *reduce* the amount of trash and litter we produce if we paid closer attention to the materials we buy, especially packaging. If we can *reuse* something, we won't need to throw it away. If we can *recycle* it, then we'll be contributing to the sustainable use of our natural resources. By using the same materials over and over to make new products, we won't be using up the limited quantities of these materials on our planet. Instead, we'll be maintaining these resources for future generations.

A worker takes apart cathode ray tube (CRT) computer monitors to prepare them for recycling at a factory in Wales, UK.

The biggest challenge is to get people to understand and care about the problem. Many people would rather buy disposable packaging because it's convenient. They don't want to clean containers. Some people even resist recycling. Mostly, they just don't think about it.

There are fines for depositing too much waste into landfills, so many cities require or at least encourage recycling. Some recycling centers even pay people to bring in their cans and bottles. Recycling really does help keep at least some materials from ending up as litter or going to landfills.

CHEWING AND CHUCKING

ABC (Already Been Chewed) gum is a major problem, especially in cities. If you've ever stepped or sat in it, you know what a sticky, yucky mess it is! Discarded chewed gum takes up to five years to biodegrade, or decompose naturally. It costs about three times as much to remove a chewed piece of gum as it did to buy it in the first place! Some countries are considering taxing gum to help pay for cleaning it up. In Singapore—a nation known for its strict laws and clean cities—it is illegal to chew gum unless you have a prescription from your doctor or dentist.

A city worker uses steam-cleaning equipment to remove chewing gum from the pavement.

Cigarette butts float in a puddle. This unsightly form of litter places a burden on drainage and sewage systems. It is also probably a lot more common than you might think. Every year about 4.5 trillion cigarette butts are dropped in the world!

CAREER PROFILE

DIGGING CONTAMINATION: ENVIRONMENTAL CONSTRUCTION, DEMOLITION, AND SPECIALIZED TRUCKING

I was raised on a dairy farm, so being around heavy equipment and doing repair work on my own was a way of life. After taking some classes on handling hazardous materials, I decided to start my own environmental cleanup business in 1995. Today, I operate bulldozers, diggers, and other machinery. I also find projects, bid on them, and do the billing and collecting of fees. I'm pretty much a one-person show!

In my daily work, I restore contaminated sites back to their original state. This might mean something as small as cleaning up a spill after a vehicle accident. On a larger scale, it might mean razing a building, removing underground fuel storage tanks, or excavating contaminated soil.

My office is my truck! Job sites are always changing, and I get to do a lot of moving around. The best part of my job is being in places where most people are not allowed. Two of my favorite jobs were helping prepare a site for the new Harley-Davidson Museum and working on the demolition of Milwaukee County Stadium. After the ballpark was demolished, asbestos was found mixed in with everything, and we handled the transportation and management of it at the landfill. This was a very high-profile job, and I was proud to have gotten our work done on time and within budget.

With going "green" being more and more the wave of the future, more people understand that environmental issues need to be faced rather than run away from. This kind of attitude makes my job easier. It also lets me know that I can count on more work coming my way in the future!

Tage George
Owner
Underground Power Corporation
Franksville, Wisconsin

A HazMat suit is an essential part of the wardrobe in the environmental cleanup business!

What are your options if you decide to work in the recycling industry? For starters, you could sort materials at a recycling center or check in and weigh incoming materials. As a manager or supervisor, you could be responsible for repairing and maintaining equipment. Your job might be to train new employees. Perhaps you'd enjoy driving a recycling truck. Companies that produce and reuse recyclable materials need people to analyze the costs and profits. You might be responsible for recycling materials that need special handling, such as electronics. Local governments and recycling companies both need creative designers of Web sites, advertising, and other materials to persuade people to recycle.

Calling All Creative People!

Thinking of ways to prevent litter is the perfect career for people who are creative and persuasive. Many people won't do anything about litter unless they understand the problem and see why they need to care about the outcome.

A day in the life and death of an underground storage tank (UST). Top: A UST is shown in the early stages of being dug up. Its exterior shows signs of leakage from the fuel that had been stored inside it. Middle: A UST that has been broken up is being dug out of the ground. The surrounding soil shows clear signs of contamination from the leaky tank. Parts of the excavating equipment used in the dig are also visible. Bottom: A fully excavated UST is loaded up and ready to be broken up and disposed of. The hole in its side was created by the scoop on the excavator.

OCEAN LITTER—WILL YOU HELP SOLVE THIS HORRIFIC PROBLEM?

Most people don't realize how much plastic trash lands in the ocean instead of being recycled or even going to a landfill. Entire beaches and vast areas of the ocean itself are covered with debris, much of it plastic. Birds and animals mistake it for food. A plastic bag bobbing on the surface can look as if it's alive. It is estimated that 100,000 marine mammals and one million sea birds die every year from swallowing or getting entangled in ocean litter.

Ocean litter comes from both land and sea sources. Land sources include trash left by beachgoers and litter blown or washed from landfills into rivers or streams to be washed into the ocean. Sea sources are primarily boats: shipping lines, cruise lines, fishing boats, and small pleasure craft. Many shipping lines and cruise lines now have rules controlling the dumping of their ships' garbage. Both have been hiring people to work on creating programs to manage their practices. They are also hiring people to publicize their efforts and to monitor the practices of their crews and passengers.

You could make good use of your interest in art, graphic design, or writing. Media and the spoken word are powerful tools, too.

Recycling is a growing industry. In recent years, scientists have developed materials that biodegrade readily. There's always a place for a product that costs even less and is better for the environment. From researching to developing advertising and public-service campaigns to encouraging recycling—if you care about these issues, the career you choose will allow you to make a difference.

This seagull picked up its plastic collar by reaching through it to pick up food. The six-pack ring may have been on the beach, floating on the water, or even in a landfill. A bird or animal tangled like this will almost certainly starve to death.

Coal Mining—Strips, Pits, and Reclamation

Our dependence upon fossil fuels has given us a huge appetite for coal. More than 40 percent of the world's electricity comes from coal-burning power plants. Coal powers other industries, too, and is often used to heat buildings as well. In 2006, worldwide coal consumption was 6.7 billion tons (6.1 metric tons).

Coal is taken from the ground either through shafts drilled underground or from open pits on the surface. More than 60 percent is taken from the surface. Various metal ores such as copper, gold, iron, and aluminum also are mined from open pits.

Can It Be Fixed?

In the United States, the Surface Mining Control and Reclamation Act of 1977 (SMCRA) set standards for reclaiming mined lands. Now, mining companies have to fix the land. Obviously, the land can never go back to being exactly as it was. A mountaintop or valley can't be replaced. Some problems can be reduced by returning topsoil and replanting native plants. In time and with help, the land may become a healthy ecosystem once again.

Above: Mining equipment removes coal from an open mine. Surface mining includes strip mining, mountain removal mining, and open pit mining. All of these methods take their toll on the landscape and native wildlife.

Below: A long line of monster dump trucks drives down into an open pit mine to pick up their next load. Note how huge they are compared to the pick-up truck. Surface mining usually involves the use of explosives and giant heavy equipment to create openings in Earth's surface and to haul off coal or mineral ores. Trees, plants, and waste from the mines are often bulldozed and dumped into nearby valleys and streams. Some abandoned open pit mines may become landfills, but many areas that were once covered with forests and other ecosystems are left barren or turned into fields of scrubby grass.

HABITAT LOSS—THE GREATEST THREAT TO WILDLIFE SURVIVAL

When an ecosystem is changed by human activity, it may no longer be able to support all the plants and animals that live there.

Habitat loss may occur when people cut down trees or fill in wetlands to make room for development. Habitats may also become fragmented when roads or dams disrupt wildlife or interfere with migratory routes. Damage created by pollution can also lead to the degrading of habitats.

It is sometimes possible to reverse habitat loss. Even better, of course, would be to prevent it from happening at all. The National Parks Conservation Association (NPCA) is an example of an organization dedicated to reversing and preventing habitat loss. NPCA staff work with the National Park Service to address land management issues.

An NPCA project might reverse habitat loss by removing all traces of a road cutting through a wilderness area. An even larger project might be to return the path of a river to its natural flow pattern.

The NPCA also keeps the public informed about challenges such as budget cuts and pollution issues. Its staff includes experts in topics ranging from business management to the impact of climate change on national parks. Among the wide range of jobs are managers, project leaders, fundraisers, consultants, researchers, team coordinators, and media people.

Roadways, railroads, or other human-made pathways break up the natural ecosystems through which they travel. They also interfere with natural habitats and species in other ways. The darkened soil and gravel shown here is a result of the release of fuel from locomotives traveling along a stretch of railroad tracks. Such releases contribute to habitat loss by contaminating soil and underlying groundwater.

Reclaiming former mining sites is an ongoing project. It calls for effective methods of restoring soil, water, plant and animal life, and more. Some U.S. states and Canadian provinces have separate agencies that deal with mine site reclamation. In Montana, for example, the staff of the Mine Waste Cleanup Bureau (MWCB) includes scientists in many fields, especially geology, hydrology, and biology. Also on the staff are archaeologists and cartographers. Archaeologists study past cultures based on objects they left behind. Cartographers create charts and maps. The MWCB hires lawyers to give legal advice about mining and environmental laws. The process of reclamation involves numerous workers, in both planning and carrying out the project. Just a few of the specific careers include mine restoration specialists, natural resource specialists, engineers with various specialties, field technicians, equipment operators, and work crews.

Blausteinsee (Blue Stone Lake), in Germany, is a highly successful example of mine site reclamation. The former coal mining pit has been converted into a popular recreation area.

WATCH YOUR FINGERS!

Just how much trouble can one fish cause? Plenty, if it happens to be a snakehead.

A voracious hunter armed with shark-like teeth, a snakehead will lash out at anything, including people. Some species grow up to 3 feet (1 m) long and weigh more than 13 pounds (6 kilograms). The snakehead is so manacing-looking and dangerous that two of its nicknames are "Frankenfish" and "Fishzilla."

Snakeheads are designed to survive. They adapt easily, eating just about anything. They can survive out of water as long as three days. They use a wriggling motion to travel on land. Worst of all, they reproduce at a rate that some wildlife biologists call "astonishing." If snakeheads get into a freshwater ecosystem, they take over, killing off the competition and rearranging the food chain. When they compete with largemouth bass, a popular sport and food fish, the bass lose. So does the ecosystem.

Snakeheads come from Asia and Africa, but they are creating an environmental crisis in freshwater ponds, lakes, and rivers around the world. They are just one example of thousands of invasive species, most of them introduced by humans, that get into ecosystems where they don't belong and take over.

Residents and Aliens

Native plants and animals are those that naturally belong in an ecosystem, without the help of humans. Invasive species are those that have somehow gotten into an ecosystem where they don't belong. In a balanced ecosystem, every species has everything it needs. Predators and other factors keep the population size to what the system can handle. When an invasive species moves in, it competes with the native species. There is not enough food, water, or oxygen for everyone to survive. In time, one species will dominate others. Too often, it's the native species that lose and die out.

Above: Hitchhikers like zebra mussels commonly attach to a boat in one lake and hop a ride to the next one. As shown in this photo, they also clog water pipes, including those at power stations. First recorded in North America in 1988, these invaders are thought to have entered the Great Lakes on a ship from Europe.

If the habitat doesn't have the right predators to keep the invader population under control, the invasives will keep reproducing and change the entire ecosystem.

If you enjoy the excitement of a hunt, you might find that a career dealing with invasives is perfect for you. Once an invasive species is established, it can be very difficult to get rid of. Removal of invasives may be part of the job description of park employees. It may also be done by field biologists and technicians working at a wildlife preserve. At the research level, scientists work to find the most effective ways to restore ecological balance.

Companies specializing in the removal of invasives operate regionally, nationally, and even worldwide. Full-time and seasonal jobs include field supervisors and workers, heavy equipment operators, and restoration ecologists. Also needed are management, marketing, support staff, and sales people. Some companies offer opportunities for young students or trainees to gain valuable work experience, usually for a limited period of time and for little or no pay, as interns.

Remediation includes reestablishing native species and continuing to monitor the area. Preventing further spreading will require people to develop and enforce guidelines or laws. Also needed are people to design and produce informational materials.

Cane toads were originally introduced to parts of the United States and other countries as a way of controlling sugar cane pests. The toads' numbers have increased dramatically. They have become pests themselves, preying upon and competing with native species. These invaders can secrete a poisonous venom, which makes them a danger to natural predators, pets, and other animals.

Kudzu, a quick-growing climbing plant, was introduced into the United States to help control soil erosion. In its native Asian habitat, freezing temperatures kept it under control. In the warmer climate of the southern United States, however, little can stop it from taking over—as it has here, in this woodland near Atlanta, Georgia.

DEALING WITH DISASTERS

Y ou've seen the images on the news. An earthquake strikes hard, followed by a tsunami. Weeks of wildfires consume thousands of acres of forest. A river floods, leaving communities and farmlands under several feet of water. Buildings, infrastructure such as railroads, highways, and electrical grids, are knocked out of commission or even destroyed.

Burning houses and wrecked ships are piled in a mass of debris amid the ruins of Kisenuma, Japan, in March 2011. The devasting earthquake and ensuing tsunami combined to create one of the most horrific natural disasters in the recorded history of our planet.

Help at All Levels

When a disaster affects human lives, there is an immediate need for help. The rescue, medical treatment, and safety of the victims are top priorities. The next step is bringing in life-sustaining supplies of food and water. If houses are destroyed, or if it isn't safe or possible for people to go back home, they'll need shelter, too.

As things settle down, the images fade away, replaced by other news. But the disaster is far from over. It can take a long time for people and places to recover. Damage to the environment needs to be

"We will make sure this place returns to the way it used to be. ... Everyone will work together and clean up this mess."

Mutsuko Ishino, Earthquake/tsunami survivor (quoted in *The Washington Post*, March 16, 2011)

NATURAL PROTECTION— HELP WANTED!

Hurricane Katrina struck the U.S. Gulf Coast in 2005. It caused 800 deaths and was the costliest hurricane on record at the time.

During the storm, a 29-foot (9 m)-tall storm surge of water came up the Mississippi River. It broke through the protective levees around New Orleans. Eventually, 80 percent of the city was under water.

If there had been wetlands at the mouth of the Mississippi, they would have acted like a sponge, soaking up wind and rain as it moved up the river. But over one million acres (405,000 hectares) of wetlands had been wiped out as a result of changes purposely made to the land at the mouth, or delta.

These changes were done to make the river more accessible for people. Channels were dug deeper so ships could get to New Orleans. The wetlands were seriously eroded by the changes to the river's natural flow. The problem was made worse by channels for oil and gas pipelines dug right through the marshes. Saltwater came up the channels and killed the freshwater grasses.

There is little doubt that the wetlands could have protected New Orleans. They need to be reestablished as soon as possible. Workers will be needed to perform the following jobs: promoting changes to government officials; planning, engineering, designing, planting, growing, maintaining, and monitoring the restored region; publicity, education, and more.

Floodwaters cover a highway in the aftermath of Hurricane Katrina, which struck the Gulf Coast in 2005. Katrina was one of the most powerful and costly hurricanes on record. The damage it caused was made even worse because most wetlands that would have absorbed some of the impact of wind and water had been removed.

dealt with, too. Cleaning up can be a matter of days, weeks, months, or years. Restoration and re-greening may take even longer.

The faster and better the damage is cleaned up, the sooner the environment can reestablish its natural balance. In some cases, damage is so great that the environment is changed forever.

Nature Isn't Always Nice

Earthquakes happen. So do floods, hurricanes, tornadoes, tsunamis, cyclones, volcanic eruptions, mudslides, and avalanches. Like it or not, these events are all part of what naturally takes place on our planet. Nature has an amazing ability to recover from its own damage and move on.

The natural world is not designed to stay exactly the same year after year, century after century. In the natural order of things, a burned forest reseeds and new plants grow. A flooding river deposits fresh topsoil on surrounding fields. Animal populations adjust to losses and repopulate the area. It won't be exactly the same as it was, but in time it will be healthy and balanced once again.

People in New Orleans demonstrate to call attention to the need for restoration of wetlands and building of levees strong enough to withstand even the most powerful hurricanes. The Stop the Flooding Coalition Rally was scheduled on a day when former President George W. Bush visited New Orleans. The goal was to draw his attention, as well as that of national and state officials, to the importance of providing funds for these projects and making them a priority.

Nature recovers and builds out of its own damaged state, as shown here with this pine forest growing and reseeding itself in volcanic ash.

OIL-SPILL OPPORTUNITIES

In addition to throngs of volunteers, an oil spill brings out people with all sorts of specialties, training, and experience. We learned this during the *Exxon Valdez* oil spill in Alaska in 1989 and in 2010, during the BP oil disaster in the Gulf of Mexico. Equipment designed especially for oil cleanup is brought in and operated. Among the scientists are chemists, hydrologists, ecologists, marine biologists, and geologists. Also on board are experts on fish, birds, sea mammals, invertebrates, wetlands, and more.

Also needed are people who know how to treat oily birds or get tar out of small pools filled with seawater, called tidal pools, without doing further damage. We learn a little more from each oil spill about what works best to help the environment recover. Long after the area looks clean again, researchers are hard at work. Some test for possible damage on the ocean floor or monitor plant and animal populations to see how well they are coming back. Others analyze the effects of the chemicals used to disperse the oil to see if they helped or caused further damage.

An oil containment boom put in place by U.S. Navy divers and salvage personnel surrounds New Harbor Island, Louisiana, protecting it from a massive oil spill in the Gulf of Mexico in 2010. These booms are designed to absorb oil as well as block it. They can also be used to contain smaller spills.

U.S. Environmental Services workers set up a boom in the Gulf Coast off of Louisiana. This boom was used to protect environmentally sensitive areas from oil released during the BP disaster.

Putting People in the Picture

When a flood destroys homes and affects the way people live, restoration usually means trying to fix or rebuild everything so it looks normal again. Some remediation might be done, such as dredging or building levees, to protect the community if another floods hits. If the floodwaters were polluted with toxic chemicals, the mud left behind can't just be put back in the fields or the river. It will need to be hauled away to be treated or disposed of safely. Successful cleanup after a natural disaster includes restoration of the environment. Taking on such a huge task puts to work people with skills ranging from operating digging equipment to engineering, soil and water research and analysis, and hazardous waste disposal.

Wildfire—Good or Bad?

As we watch the fury of a wildfire on TV or see the charred remains of people's homes, it's hard to think of a wildfire as anything but a disaster. When people's homes, property, and even lives are at stake, a wildfire IS a disaster. In many habitats, however, fires are part of nature's cycle of growth. They are a way of cleaning up the area so that new life can begin. In fact, the seeds of some trees and plants need the heat of a fire in order to sprout. If it weren't for fire occasionally clearing out a forest, new young trees wouldn't have the space or light to compete and grow.

In the aftermath of Hurricane Katrina in 2005, safely disposing of hazardous materials was a huge challenge facing cleanup planners and workers. Shown above are some of the hundreds of thousands of refrigerators, stoves, washers, and dryers collected at a landfill for disposal and recycling. Food left in the refrigerators was placed in plastic bags and disposed of in another landfill.

Workers in HazMat suits take samples from recovered drums with unknown chemicals in them to determine the best way to dispose of them. At this site alone, contractors hired by the U.S. Environmental Protection Agency (EPA) processed 10,000 drums in the aftermath of Hurricane Katrina.

41

People once thought that any wildfire was a bad thing. They were put out as quickly as possible, rather than letting them burn themselves out. Shrubs and dead plant material build up on the forest floor. As a result, fires happened less often, but when they did, they were much more destructive. Now we know that wise management includes allowing these areas to burn every so often.

Fire ecologists study the origin of wildfire and its effect on an ecosystem. They look at the history of fire in an area, including how often they happen, their intensity, and how much fuel is consumed. Communication skills are also important. People need help understanding that fire isn't always a bad thing!

Superfunds to the Rescue

The U.S. Superfund program is designed to clean up the worst hazardous waste sites. Likely candidates are closed dumps and landfills, abandoned mines, old factories and refineries, and military sites. Superfunds are supervised by the EPA. They cannot be used on sites that are still active.

A burned forest in Grand Canyon National Park, Arizona. Forest fires can be one way that nature "cleans house," clearing the land of dead plant matter and other debris so new life can enter the wooded habitat.

Whenever possible, the polluter pays. If necessary, the government takes legal action to make former owners and users of the site either do the cleanup or pay for it. If the polluters can't be found, the costs are paid from a "Superfund." The money comes from a tax on chemical and petroleum companies.

The Superfund program was established in response to the desperate need at the chemically polluted Love Canal. Sites are now evaluated, selected, and given a spot on the NPL (National Priorities List). More than 40,000 hazardous waste sites across the United States and its territories have been identified. About 1,000 of these have been selected as priority sites.

LOVE CANAL

Before the late 1970s, the Love Canal section of Niagara Falls, New York, looked like any other suburban-style neighborhood with nice houses and a school. The problem was that it was built on top of a dump. First the city, then the U.S. Army dumped its waste into an empty canal. A chemical company filled it with 21,000 tons (19,051 metric tons) of chemicals and then covered it with dirt. The residents had no idea about the history of their land. They were concerned about pools of oil and colored liquids forming in basements and yards. A newspaper reporter decided to investigate, going door to door asking questions. He found so many birth defects, illnesses, and other problems that he advised the residents to form a protest group.

At first, neither the government nor the chemical company paid much attention. Finally, an Environmental Protection Agency (EPA) official visited and recognized the emergency. Children and pregnant women were advised to leave immediately. The homeowners wanted to get out, but they couldn't sell their homes. Who would buy them?

Residents finally got action when Love Canal hit the headlines. Medical research showed the chemicals could cause cancer or genetic damage. Until then, federal funds had been used only for natural disasters. In 1978, however, President Jimmy Carter said they should be used on Love Canal. The government bought the homes of 800 families and relocated them.

An aerial photo of the Love Canal region of Niagara Falls, New York. On the left side of the photo is the Hooker Chemical plant complex, which began dumping toxic waste in the 1940s. Prior to that, both the city and the military had used the area as a chemical dumping ground and landfill.

BORING DOWN ON CONTAMINATION: RESEARCH ENGINEER

When I was little, I loved digging big holes in the ground. I'd stand inside, fascinated by the different layers of rock and soil.

One of the highlights of my career involved working on a gasoline leak from storage tanks into the surrounding soil and down to the water table below. It was traveling rapidly toward the river. Vapors were seeping out beneath homes in the neighborhood.

First we drilled boreholes into the contaminated soil. Then we used a vacuum to draw out the vapors. As the vapors were sucked out, oxygen was drawn in. We discovered that bringing in more oxygen increased the ability of natural bacteria in the soil to consume the gasoline. One of my colleagues and I got credit for inventing this process.

One memorable trip took me to the former Soviet Union. We were asked to offer advice on waste management and pollution issues. They took us to Chernobyl, the site of a nuclear reactor meltdown seven years earlier in Soviet Ukraine.

The best part of my work is being outside, exchanging ideas, solving problems, and helping people. My advice is to be broad in your work experience, even while you are still in school. Get a really good scientific background and be flexible, but keep driving toward your areas of interest.

Doug Ely
Research Engineer
Chevron
Richmond, California

Working on Superfund Sites

The EPA hires companies, not individuals, to work on Superfund sites. If you are interested in working on Superfund projects, you might seek employment at a company that provides any of a wide variety of environmental cleanup services. These may include environmental consulting, investigation, management, technology, monitoring, and engineering and design. Other services include renting, monitoring, and operating construction equipment; on-site water and soil treatment; soil excavation; and laboratory sampling and analysis. The treatment, decontamination, disposal, and transportation of hazardous waste are also high on the list of jobs available on Superfund sites.

In 1989, an explosion inside the Chernobyl power plant in then-Soviet Ukraine released highly radioactive material. It drifted over the western Soviet Union and parts of Europe. In the years since, 6,000 people who were exposed to the radiation as children have developed thyroid cancer. This photo shows the ghost city of Pripyat in the contaminated zone. The devastated Chernobyl nuclear reactor can be seen in the background.

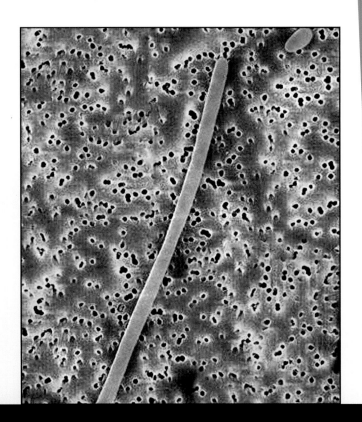

This enhanced transmission electron micrograph (TEM) shows bacteria (in pink) that are breaking down oil from the BP spill in the Gulf of Mexico. This species, which was unknown to researchers prior to the spill, has been consuming oil as far as half a mile (1 km) below the ocean's surface, and at a much faster rate than expected.

OIL-EATING BACTERIA!

What do oil and gasoline have in common with the food we eat? Both contain carbon and hydrogen, among other things. Oil in any of its many forms is toxic to us, but to certain types of bacteria, it's an appealing, life-sustaining food.

How do bacteria "eat" oil? They use oxygen from the air, water, or soil around them to break the strong bonds between the carbon and hydrogen atoms. The result is smaller molecules that the bacteria can take in to make energy and material for new cells.

Oil-eating bacteria are tremendously valuable when there is an oil spill, whether on land or water. It used to be that cleaning up oil meant hauling it away somewhere. It might also have meant using detergent chemicals that create their own problems. When bacteria consume oil, however, it's gone, period, and that's that. It's relatively fast, effective, and permanent.

Case Study: PEPCON—An Accident That Lives on

Ammonium perchlorate is a highly explosive substance used in rocket fuel for the Space Shuttle. Back in 1988, the only two plants that made it were located just 5 miles (8 km) apart in the little industrial town of Henderson, Nevada. One of these plants, PEPCON, was out in the desert well away from town. Its nearest neighbor was a marshmallow factory.

The shuttle program had been suspended in 1986 after the *Challenger* disaster, but PEPCON continued to manufacture the chemical at the same rate. There was no place to ship the chemical, so they stored it on-site in 55-gallon plastic drums.

Just before lunch on May 4, 1988, a spark from a welder started a small fire. It quickly spread, and the workers were unable to put it out. Realizing what was about to happen, they ran for their lives across the desert.

Nine million pounds (four million kilograms) of chemicals blew up during a series of deafening blasts. A visible shock wave tossed vehicles off the road, shattered windshields and windows, and buckled garage doors.

This image of a huge mushroom cloud, taken from a film clip made with a handheld camera, shows the astonishing force of the second major explosion at the PEPCON plant in 1988.

PEPCON ON VIDEO

Watch amazing firsthand videos of the PEPCON disaster at www.youtube.com/watch?v=WzPksCgnCqc

The force of the strongest blast was the same as 250 tons (227 metric tons) of TNT. It measured 3.5 on the Richter scale.

PEPCON was destroyed, and the marshmallow factory was flattened. A crater 15 feet (4.5 m) deep and 200 feet (61 m) wide marked where the explosion took place. More than 300 people were hurt, but amazingly only two people were killed. The other rocket fuel plant was damaged by the force of the PEPCON blast, but thankfully it did not blow up.

After the Blast

The immediate concern for environmental damage was chemical fallout. Luckily, the wind was light that day. Health officials said lives were saved because of the way the winds blew and dispersed the chemicals.

No one knows exactly how much perchlorate was spread across the surrounding land. It is soluble (easily dissolved in water). Anything that landed on the surface was probably washed away by rain or seeped down through the sandy soil. If anything, only small traces would have been left behind.

The site of the blast was cleaned up and then sat vacant for several years. The area was rapidly growing, however. New homes and buildings spread out across the desert. Today a business development sits where PEPCON once was.

PREVENTING PROBLEMS AS A CAREER

Risk management is a growing career field. State and government agencies, private companies, industries, and environmental consulting firms all hire risk managers. Risk managers advise companies and agencies on how to keep workplaces safe from toxins and pollutants. They help their employers develop a plan to come into compliance with environmental regulations. Their goal is to prevent practices, accidents, and mistakes that could cause harm to people, property, or the environment.

Risk management professionals spend time at their desks, but they also must be able to go out into the field to assess the extent to which companies and government agencies are complying with environmental regulations.

BROWNFIELD SUCCESS STORIES

The best use for land isn't always to keep it wild. Re-greening can also prepare a site to be put back into use.

A brownfield is a contaminated piece of property. Left untreated, it could become a threat to human health and the environment. Developing it could help the local economy by bringing in new business or affordable housing. It could also create jobs. But it needs to be cleaned up before it can be used.

Once a brownfield site is selected for development, environmental engineers study it and form a plan to remediate it. It is cleared of any debris or trash. Specialists come in to clean up the soil, groundwater, surface water, or anything else needed. Then the site can be leased or sold, and building can begin.

In Charlottetown, Prince Edward Island, 23 affordable rental apartments were built on the brownfield site of a former public works garage. It worked out very well. Now several other properties in the neighborhood are doing likewise.

In Hamilton, Ontario, 568 residences and several businesses are being built on a brownfield steel foundry site. During the clearing and cleaning of the site, soils were sorted to find recyclable materials. Costs were reduced, as was the amount sent to a landfill.

It Isn't Over Yet

The most serious impact has been—and continues to be—on the water supply. Perchlorate seeped down through the ground until it reached the aquifer. From there, it spread out across the valley, contaminating well water. Finally, it reached Lake Mead, an immense reservoir supplying water to about 30 million people in the southwestern United States.

Further studies showed that perchlorate got into the groundwater not so much as the result of the explosions, but more because of spills and careless handling at both plants over the years.

This brownfield site was once home to a company that manufactured car frames in Milwaukee, Wisconsin. It is now being redeveloped for commercial and industrial use. As part of the soil and groundwater cleanup, this 40,000-gallon underground storage tank (UST) has been removed and is about to be cut up and disposed of. The soil surrounding the tank, also shown in this photo, has been contaminated with fuel that leaked from the tank. Along with adjacent groundwater, the soil will have to be removed and remediated.

In fact, it turned out that contamination from the other plant was even worse than from PEPCON. Perchlorate contamination continues to be a problem both for local wells and for Lake Mead.

Active in the Aftermath

Think about all the people involved in cleaning up and remediating after an incident such as the PEPCON disaster. Some are immediately on the scene determining the amount of damage and danger. Some figure out what needs to be done, and how to go about doing it. Others do the work of cleaning up the site. Some test for contamination and analyze the results.

People have been remediating and monitoring this disaster for more than 20 years, and there is still work to do. PEPCON is far from the only accident dealing with perchlorates or other substances that cause ongoing environmental damage. In addition to the standard jobs of most re-greening situations, scientists with specific training such as chemists, hydrologists, geologists, and biologists would be needed. Of course, people from various local and national environmental agencies would be involved. Where might you be? Can you picture yourself responding to this challenge?

CAREER PROFILE

KEEPING A WATCH ON RADIATION: CHEMICAL AND MATERIALS ANALYST

I prepare environmental samples to be analyzed for radiation. Most of these samples are taken from water, the atmosphere, and farmland. I am also on call for the Georgia Emergency Management Agency (GEMA) and act as a backup technician for the state's Mobile Radiation Lab (MRL).

We analyze the samples as part of the Environmental Protection Agency (EPA) monitoring program. Sometimes I get to test my skills with dangerous radioactive samples. We call these training exercises, and we use the samples to help us simulate nuclear accidents and nuclear or terrorist attacks that release radioactive materials. I enjoy doing the lab work, analyzing data, and sharing data and research with other EPA labs. I also enjoy the field work and training exercises.

I studied geology, biology, and, in graduate school, geochemistry. Having a good background in science and environmental sciences is important in my career.

I don't think that burning fossil fuels is a real solution to providing for our energy needs. So I'm an advocate for clean, well-regulated nuclear power. I hope that one day we can finally create efficient nuclear fusion.

Richard Jakiel
Chemical and Materials Analyst
Department of Natural Resources,
Environmental Radiation Protection
Atlanta, Georgia

CHAPTER 5

PUT IT BACK! HABITAT RESTORATION

It's one thing to restore a wilderness environment after a disaster. What if the area has been drastically changed, or developed, and is now being used for something else? It can be difficult and costly to re-green an area if it means removing the changes and returning the area to its natural state.

Salmon vs. Electric Power

The Condit Dam on the White Salmon River in the state of Washington is 125 feet (38 m) tall. It blocks salmon migration to 13 miles (21 km) of spawning grounds. If the fish could get through, they could produce as many as 10,000 offspring every year.

The Condit Dam on the White Salmon River in Washington. Its owner, the PacifiCorp power company, has requested that the federal government approve a demolition project that would be, to date, the largest dam removal project in U.S. history.

The dam produces enough electricity for 13,000 homes. That's not a lot, compared to other hydroelectric dams. The Condit doesn't provide water for irrigation, nor is it designed to prevent flooding. The owners looked at both sides of the situation. They decided that it would be better to remove the dam than try to make a way for the salmon to swim upstream. The fish are more valuable than the electricity. The dam is scheduled to come down in 2011.

It took more than ten years of planning, surveys, analysis, and reports to meet the legal requirements before removing the dam was approved. The next step, demolition, requires an additional work force to tear down, clean up, deal with wildlife, and, of course, continue with paperwork, surveys, monitoring, and such. After that, restoration can begin. That will be the work of ecologists, environmental engineers, and many more, including people simply willing to dig in.

A young Coho salmon. The Coho is one of the species whose numbers will be restored in the White Salmon River following the removal of the Condit Dam.

RESTORATION COMPANY

The staff of an environmental restoration company typically includes people skilled in science, horticulture (growing plants), landscape architecture, technology, and design. Work crew jobs range from operating heavy machinery in fragile areas to restoring alpine streams and endangered plant habitats.

In a process called soil bioengineering, live native plants are used to control erosion, stabilize slopes and stream banks, and restore wildlife habitats. Soil bioengineering combines the skills of soil scientists, landscape architects, horticulturists, and civil, hydrological, and geotechnical engineers.

Success Story: Re-Greening the Giacomini Wetlands

Tomales Bay is a narrow saltwater bay running from north to south along the San Andreas Fault in northern California. To the west is the Point Reyes Peninsula, much of which is now part of the Point Reyes National Seashore. Fresh water from Lagunitas Creek flows into the bay at the south end. For thousands of years, it made its way through wetlands to mix with the salt water at high tide.

Then, in the 1940s, earthen levees were constructed to channel the creek directly into the bay. The wetlands, now dry, became pasture for the Giacomini dairy ranch. The water quality in Tomales Bay gradually got worse and worse. Sediment built up, and invasive species, most of them introduced by humans over the years, moved in. Plants and animals that had relied on the wetland ecosystem disappeared. The artificial channel dug for Lagunitas Creek could not begin to do what the wetlands had done naturally for hundreds of years.

When the national seashore was established in 1962, many of the dairy ranches were allowed to continue operating. In 2000, the Giacomini family sold its land to the National Park Service.

Crew members work on a riverbed as part of the Harris River restoration project in Alaska. The project aims to reverse the effects of logging, road construction, and other human activity, as well as some natural events, on fish and other wildlife that are part of this aquatic habitat.

The dream of turning 550 acres (223 hectares) of pastureland back into wetlands went into action. The earthen levees were removed. Creek banks were stabilized against erosion. Refuges for wildlife, especially endangered species, were created above the high tide line. Native species were brought in as invasive plants were taken out.

An Unforgettable Moment

On October 25, 2008, the wetlands-to-be were ready to meet the saltwater again. One final scoop was taken out of the levee holding back the saltwater. Onlookers clapped and cheered as water from Tomales Bay poured in through the gap. Nature could now go to work to reestablish the wetlands.

Almost immediately, waterfowl came back in greater numbers. Within a year, water quality in the bay improved dramatically. Today, reeds, rushes, and other wetland plants are moving in. Their leaves and roots provide shade and shelter for fish and aquatic vertebrates.

"It was one of those times in life when you know you have made a difference. It was more than doing a good job."

Wetland ecologist and project manager Lorraine Parsons, reflecting on watching the water return to the Giacomini Wetlands

WHY WETLANDS?

Wetlands are soggy land areas such as marshes, swamps, and bogs. Typically, they support a unique, diverse mix of plant and animal life. They purify water that moves through them and serve as a natural flood control system. Animals including fish, sharks, and seals rely on wetlands as a nursery for their young.

Unfortunately, many wetlands have been drained for real estate development or pasture. Others have been dredged to form recreational lakes or deeper channels for shipping. By the 1990s, half of the world's wetlands had been drained.

53

VEGETATION/WETLAND ECOLOGIST AND RESTORATION PROJECT MANAGER

I've followed a winding career path. Originally, I planned to be a journalist. When my college program required a second area of study, I chose biology.

After graduation, I got a job with a newspaper. My science background led me to science and business writing, and I found that I liked writing even better than reporting. While writing for an environmental journal, I interviewed a leading wetlands restoration expert. She inspired me to do graduate study.

Next came a consulting job in natural resource management, including restoration and monitoring. Then I applied for my current job in the Point Reyes National Seashore.

Sometimes the people I supervise and I work in the office. Sometimes we're out in the field. My team includes a restoration ecologist, another wetland ecologist, a biotechnician, a fire ecologist, and several interns.

My responsibilities for vegetation management include managing existing communities, removing invasives, and protecting rare and endangered plants.

The best part of my job is preventing species extinction. Right now we're protecting the Sonoma spineflower, a plant so rare that only this one colony is known to exist.

I recommend looking for internships for on-the-job experience and to find out what really interests you. Environmental science is an up-and-coming field because of all the interest in restoration.

Lorraine Parsons
Point Reyes National Seashore
Vegetation/Wetland Ecologist and Project Manager
Marin County, California

The re-greening of the Giacomini Wetlands is just one example of a successful restoration. It took ten years to plan and carry out what needed to be done, but what a victory! Other similar restorations are in the planning stage or taking place in many locations. The need for these projects may be the result of pollution, human impact, accident, or natural disaster. In the future, there will be more and more such work as we recognize the importance of cleaning up damaged areas of the environment and keeping it healthy.

Who Does the Restoring?

What does all this work mean for you and your future career? Take a look at the dramatic and moving video account of the

Marin County (California) Conservation Corps crew members install protective enclosures around freshwater plants in marshland that is part of the Giacomini Wetlands. The enclosures are designed to keep out birds that feed on marsh plants.

Giacomini Wetland Restoration Project (www.openroad.tv/video.php?vid=399). You will see people being interviewed, as well as people gathered around working on the project and waiting for the dramatic moment when the excavator scoops out the levee holding back the water. Park superintendents, wetland ecologists, maintenance chiefs, engineers, Web page engineers, environmental monitors, volunteer coordinators, and designers, graphic artists, and printers of community communication materials each had a hand in the project. The work was done over a ten-year period and included careful planning, site preparation, publicity, and hands-on labor. In the future, some will continue to monitor and maintain the site. If restoration is the work for you, you'll have many choices to pick from!

Project Manager Lorraine Parsons gives a status update on the Giacomini Wetlands project.

A work crew from a company specializing in open land management and restoration replants native vegetation. Once established, these plants will speed up the process of regrowth and provide shelter to encourage native species to return.

What Do I Do Now?

Re-greening is a growing field, encompassing many job possibilities. New challenges mean opportunities to create new job descriptions. So what do you do now?

One thing you can do is take all the math, science, and tech courses you can. That's a great way to find out what particular areas you like and have a talent for. The interests you develop in school in the next few years may well guide you into the career of your choice.

Math and science courses are also necessary if you want to have a more hands-on role in re-greening damaged areas. You never know what background knowledge you might need during a restoration project. You may even discover that a math or science course you took may give you an advantage for a particular job or job advancement. The more knowledge you have, the better prepared you will be to pursue the career of your dreams.

In the field, the lab, or the classroom, taking science and math courses is a great way to lay some groundwork for a career in re-greening the environment!

Most jobs require a minimum of high school education. For some, that's enough—plus, perhaps, training or coursework suited to the particular job. Others require an associate (two-year) or university (four-year) degree. Some require a postgraduate degree. Many jobs require experience working in the field.

If you choose to study a broad field of science, you will find more and more areas of special interest as you go. For example, a Geology degree could lead to specializing in decontaminating soil or sampling the ocean floor. A degree in Engineering could lead you into something you never expected! Our understanding of the environment is changing and growing. Job opportunities are changing right along with it.

A hydrogeologist discusses soil and groundwater test results with people at the home office. He works for an environmental services company. His co-workers include environmental engineers, technicians, environmental scientists, technical editors, and heavy equipment operators.

A striking example of oil contaminating ground and water habitats. Cleaning it up requires teamwork and a wide range of skills in technology, science, math, and mechanics.

Here's something else to think about: Thousands of people have been out of work since the recession that began in the mid-1990s. Yet there have been many interesting, well-paying jobs available that were never taken. Why? The employers couldn't find applicants who knew enough about math, science, and technology to qualify.

Volunteering is a great way to start your re-greening career. Donate your time during the summer or while on vacation. Check out parks, volunteer agencies, and even local companies. If you hear about an environmental cleanup project, large or small, find out how you can help and join in. Every bit of experience you get is in your favor!

Be a volunteer and get your hands dirty doing environmental cleanup! From the top: cleaning oil off of a seabird in the Netherlands; students planting trees and shrubs to help stabilize banks against erosion along the Lagunitas Creek in the Giacomini Wetlands, California; picking up broken glass from a trail; and picking up litter on the beach.

START YOUR GREEN FUTURE NOW...

It's exciting to have plans and dreams for the future. It's also exciting to try new things. Here are some fun projects to help you find out what you enjoy doing and to whet your appetite for your future career.

RAISE LITTER AWARENESS

What's the litter situation at your school? Start a campaign to raise awareness and educate your fellow students (and staff). Use your creative talents to remind them where to stash the trash. If your school has a recycling program, encourage people to use it. If not, work with the administration to get such a program going.

ORGANIZE A RE-GREEN DAY

Are there beaches or parks where you live? Where do people hang out? Organize a one-day event to spruce it up. If there doesn't seem to be a need, perhaps you can plant native plants and wildflowers along the roadsides leading into town. You might want to make it an annual event, maybe part of celebrating Earth Day (April 22).

VOLUNTEER

Volunteering is one of the best ways to begin your green career. You'll gain a lot of experience and learn about re-greening the environment. Find out if there are any restoration or remediation projects planned or taking place near your home. If so, find out what you can do to help. Many local, state, and national parks have summer programs in which volunteers help with projects such as removing invasive plants, replanting areas with native plants, or rebuilding a damaged creek bed.

BE A GREEN VOICE

What kind of packaging is used in your school cafeteria, or at the snack bar if you have one? What about local fast-food restaurants? If it's the type that ends up in a landfill, speak up! First, get the facts and learn about possible alternatives. Be respectful and persuasive as you speak or write to those with authority. It's a good opportunity to practice good communication skills that may come in handy in your green career. Students like you have successfully encouraged their schools or local businesses to make changes in the materials they purchase and use. Look around your community for other opportunities to educate people about caring for the environment.

START A RE-GREEN THE ENVIRONMENT CLUB OR SERVICE GROUP

Work with your local government to identify an area that needs help right where you live! It might be removing trash dumped in a river or pond, repairing damage done by off-road vehicles, or even adopting a stretch of roadside to keep clean. While you're at it, see about replanting native plants. ALWAYS work with local authorities and/or the landowner. You'll need permission to be on the land. If you come across something hazardous, let the experts deal with it and be sure to watch and learn.

JOIN A SUPPORT ORGANIZATION

Stay informed by joining a global organization such as the World Wildlife Fund (WWF), the National Parks Conservation Association, or the Canadian Parks and Recreation Association. National parks often have community support groups, too. Many towns and cities have environmental associations. They'd appreciate your support and interest.

BE SMART, BE SAFE!

Please get permission from the adult who cares for you before making trips to new places or volunteering your free time. Always let him or her know where you are going and who you are meeting.

GROW NATIVE PLANTS

Ask the science faculty at your school or a nearby university which plants are native to your area. Watch to see when they go to seed. Collect seeds to plant and care for the seedlings. A local nursery or garden center might be able to advise you, too. You'll have plants to use for local re-greening projects.

GLOSSARY

aquifer An underground layer of rock, sand, or gravel that contains water

asthma A chronic (long-term) disease that inflames and narrows airways in the lungs, causing attacks of wheezing, coughing, tightness in the chest, and shortness of breath

biodegrade To break down or decompose naturally, especially as a result of action by bacteria and other microorganisms

brownfield Unused property that could be redeveloped or reused except that it is contaminated or potentially contaminated by pollution or a hazardous substance

cholera A serious, often deadly infectious disease causing severe diarrhea and fluid loss. Cholera is caused by eating food or drinking water contaminated by bacteria from other cholera victims.

conserve To use resources carefully and sparingly, avoiding waste; to protect from loss or harm

delta A landform at the mouth of a river where it flows into another body of water. A delta is formed from sediment deposited by the river. It is usually shaped like a triangle.

ecology The study of interactions of organisms with each other and with their environment. A scientist who studies these interactions is an ecologist.

ecosystem A complete community of living organisms and their non-living surroundings

fallout Toxic or radioactive particles that fall out of the atmosphere to the ground after an explosion

geology The study of rocks and minerals. A geologist is a scientist who specializes in rocks and minerals.

groundwater Water found underground in cracks and spaces in rock, sand, and soil. It moves slowly through (or is stored in) layers of rock, sand, and soil called aquifers.

habitat loss The destruction of natural habitat, to the point at which it can no longer support the species that live there; also known as habitat destruction

hazardous Dangerous. Hazardous waste is waste that is dangerous or potentially harmful to human health or the environment.

hydrogeologist A scientist who specializes in the position and movement of groundwater in soil and rocks under Earth's surface

hydrology The study of movement, distribution, and quality of water on Earth and in the atmosphere. A scientist who specializes in hydrology is a hydrologist.

infrastructure The basic physical structures needed for the operation of a society. Roads, buildings, railroads, and power plants are all part of a society's infrastructure.

invasive species or **invasives** Plants or animals that intrude upon a habitat or ecosystem where they do not belong, competing with the native plants or animals, and often overwhelming them

levee An embankment or ridge built to prevent the overflow of a body of water

native species Organisms that originated in, and naturally belong in, the habitat or ecosystem where they live

pollution A substance that damages or poisons the air, water, or land

preserve To keep an area exactly as it is; to protect wildlife, wildlands, or natural resources totally

Richter scale A numerical scale comparing the magnitude (intensity) of earthquakes

sediments Solid fragments of material that settle to the bottom of a body of water

smog (smoke + fog) Visible air pollution that forms a brownish-yellow haze

sustainable Capable of being continued or used with little or no long-term effect on the environment

thyroid A gland located in the base of the neck that makes and stores hormones essential to every cell in the body. Thyroid hormones help regulate growth and development, heart rate, body temperature, blood pressure, and the rate at which food is converted into energy

toxic Poisonous. A toxicologist is a scientist who specializes in poisonous substances

wetland A natural habitat of rivers, ponds, lakes, and marshes

FURTHER INFORMATION

www.unexplained-mysteries.com/viewvideo. php?id=nmU7etSYYqI&tid=119755
See the fearsome-looking snakehead, the "fishzilla" of invasive species, in action. Also see what biologists and other environmental experts are doing to try to control it.

www.freecycle.org/
Find out more about the Freecycle Network™, a grassroots global movement to keep good stuff out of landfills. You can also find if there's a group near where you live. Chances are that you'll find one!

www.watershedactivities.com/
The W.A.T.E.R. (Watershed Activities To Encourage Restoration) Web site is a collection of step-by-step instructions for simple, low-cost restoration projects that environmental groups or clubs can do. Just a few of the many projects are stream cleanups, tree planting, invasives removal, and building nest boxes.

www.epa.gov/
On this Web site for the Environmental Protection Agency (EPA) you'll find information on a wide range of environmental challenges and activity, including emergency monitoring, upcoming and ongoing projects, and Superfund sites. While you're at it, check out the air and water quality where you live.

www.ecoemploy.com/
Here's a wealth of information about preparing for, finding, and securing an environmental job in the United States or Canada.

www.goodworkcanada.ca/
Canada's green job site is loaded with information, including what's available, who's hiring, and how to go about preparing for and finding the job opportunities you are looking for.

www.sciencebuddies.org/ science-fair-projects/science_careers.shtml
Check out this excellent Web site, frequently updated with a list of careers related to science, math, technology, and engineering, including green careers. It gives details about what is involved, requirements, salary, outlook, etc. Includes videos of people doing the jobs.

www.campusaccess.com/internships/ environmental.html
Perhaps you'll find a step to your green career in this guide to environmental internship and volunteer possibilities.

www.jobcorps.gov/Libraries/Recovery/ student_one_pager.sflb
http://www.jobcorps.gov/home.aspx
See what Job Corps has to say about how to prepare for a green career.

www.epa.gov/highschool/careers.htm
A lot of resources for students looking for summer jobs, intern opportunities, fellowships, grants, and more can be found on this Web site.

INDEX

INDEX

ABOUT THE AUTHOR

Suzy Gazlay is an award-winning teacher and writer of children's nonfiction books and science songs. Her experience includes developing educational curriculum, and she frequently serves as a content and curriculum consultant. She loves being outdoors, whether it's exploring tide pools, hiking in the mountains, or working in her garden. She also enjoys singing and playing several different instruments.